T0199201

P*INKY
the M*nster
& THE SECRET GARDEN

A DAY AT THE BEACH

Written by **LINDY J**

Pinky The Monster and The Secret Garden:
A Day At The Beach

To order additional copies of this book, contact:
Xlibris
AU TFN: 1 800 844 927 (Toll Free inside Australia)
AU Local: 0283 108 187 (+61 2 8310 8187 from outside Australia)
www.xlibris.com.au
Orders@Xlibris.com.au

ISBN: Softcover   978-1-9845-0566-8
        Hardcover   978-1-9845-0567-5
        EBook   978-1-9845-0565-1

Print information available on the last page

Rev. date: 06/12/2020

Dedicated to my amazing god daughters — Annie and Tilly.
For your infectious enthusiasm and belief in Pinky the Monster
and his friends.

To my Editor Roisin Heycock.
Your guidance and belief in my book was invaluable.

To Ong Lyn-Hui from ForReal Studio.
Your incredible illustrations really bought this book to life.
Thank you.

Pinky the monster woke up
and stretched his wings.

He looked around his home, a Secret Garden.
So colourful and full of life.

Birds were singing in the trees.

The sun was shining.
"Oh my, what a wonderful day to go
to the beach!" said Pinky.

Pinky ran across the grass as fast as he could and flew off into the brilliant blue sky.

Wee...Whoo...Yippee...

In the distance Pinky saw the blue water and glistening golden sand of the beach.

"Yahoo!" Pinky sang.

Pinky tucked his special wings in tight and landed right in the middle of the beach.

He tumbled over and over again.It made him laugh so hard.

Phew thought Pinky. His wings were safe!

Waiting at the beach to play were three of his best friends:

Lucy

Rex

and Ernie

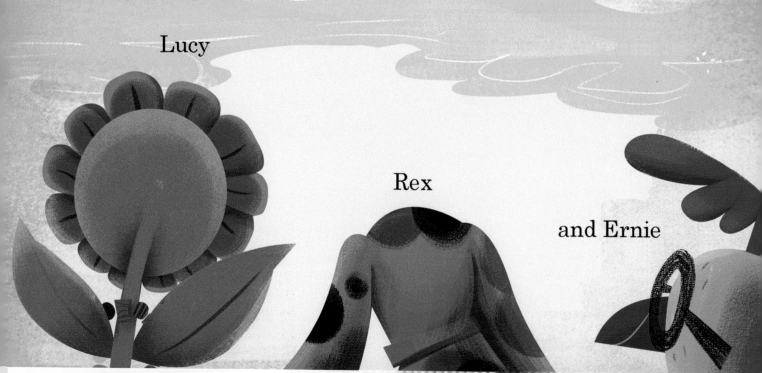

Rex was a very excitable and playful dog.

He had big long floppy ears and his fur was a mixture of white, brown and black all mixed in together.

Rex was forever tripping over his ears especially when he got excited.

Sometimes Rex wished his ears were smaller as they always seemed to get him into trouble wherever he went.

Rex saw Pinky and ran as fast as he could along the beach.

"Come on," said Rex. **"Let's play."**

Ernie was an old lazy and often grumpy chicken.

He had hardly any feathers, big red feet and a big red beak.

Ernie wished he had feathers like all the other chickens.

But his friends didn't care.

They loved him just the way he was.

Ernie found a nice shady spot under a tree
so he could watch his friends have fun.

Lucy was the most beautiful sunflower in the whole world.

Her thin, tall green body shone so bright it sparkled like diamonds, and her face was as golden as the sun.

Lucy looked just like a princess.

Everybody loved Lucy.

She was always smiling and helping her friends.

"Pinky, you're here," said Lucy. "Everyone's here."

"Let's start playing."

The four friends played and swam
at the beach all day.

Pinky could use his wings in the water
like flippers. He swam, ducked and
dived just like a dolphin.

Rex chased Pinky up and down the
beach, barking loudly and trying not
to trip over his big long, floppy ears.

All of a sudden without thinking Rex
decided to see if he could swim like
Pinky and jumped into the water.

Rex thought he could use his ears as flippers just like Pinky used his wings.

And then....

Rex felt his ears become very heavy and before he knew it he was sinking to the bottom of the ocean.

Pinky came up for air, turned around and couldn't see Rex.

"Lucy. Have you seen Rex?"

yelled Pinky.

"No, I can't see him anywhere. We have to find him," said Lucy.

"Leave it to me," said Pinky.

Pinky dived down to the bottom of the ocean looking for Rex whilst Lucy searched up and down the beach. Lucy still couldn't see Rex anywhere.

"Ernie, we have lost Rex!"

yelled Lucy.

Ernie ran down the beach without even worrying about the sand that was now stuck between the toes of his big red feet.

He needed to help find their friend Rex.

Underwater Pinky saw a large brown blob swaying to the rhythm of the ocean. He swam towards the blob and poked it.

It was REX!

Pinky grabbed Rex and swam to shore as fast as he could. Rex wasn't breathing.

Ernie slapped Rex with his big red beak!

All of a sudden Rex opened his eyes and coughed up a whole bunch of seaweed and water.

"You're **alive!**" cried Lucy in delight.
"Pinky, you saved Rex."

"What happened?"

cried Rex.

"You almost drowned. Next time you decide to go swimming don't think your ears are like flippers," said Lucy.

"I'm sorry, thank you for saving me Pinky," said Rex softly.

"I hate my ears, they are always getting me into trouble," mumbled Rex coughing up more water.

"Don't hate your ears, they make you special. No other dog has ears as wonderful as yours. Be proud of them," said Lucy.

Ernie didn't say much.
He just shook his head wondering
why Rex never thinks about what
he is about to do.

"Ugghh," thought Ernie. How am I ever
going to get all the sand out from between
the toes of my big red feet?"

"I think we should all go home before anything else happens,"
muttered Lucy.

"Come on, it's time to go," said Pinky.

Rex, Lucy and Ernie jumped on Pinky's back, held on tight and flew home, darting through tall city buildings, over big green parks and finally landing quietly in front of their home.

A Secret Garden!

The Secret Garden was so special and magical.

Waiting in the Secret Garden were some of their other friends. Ben the bee and Clara the bright green caterpillar.

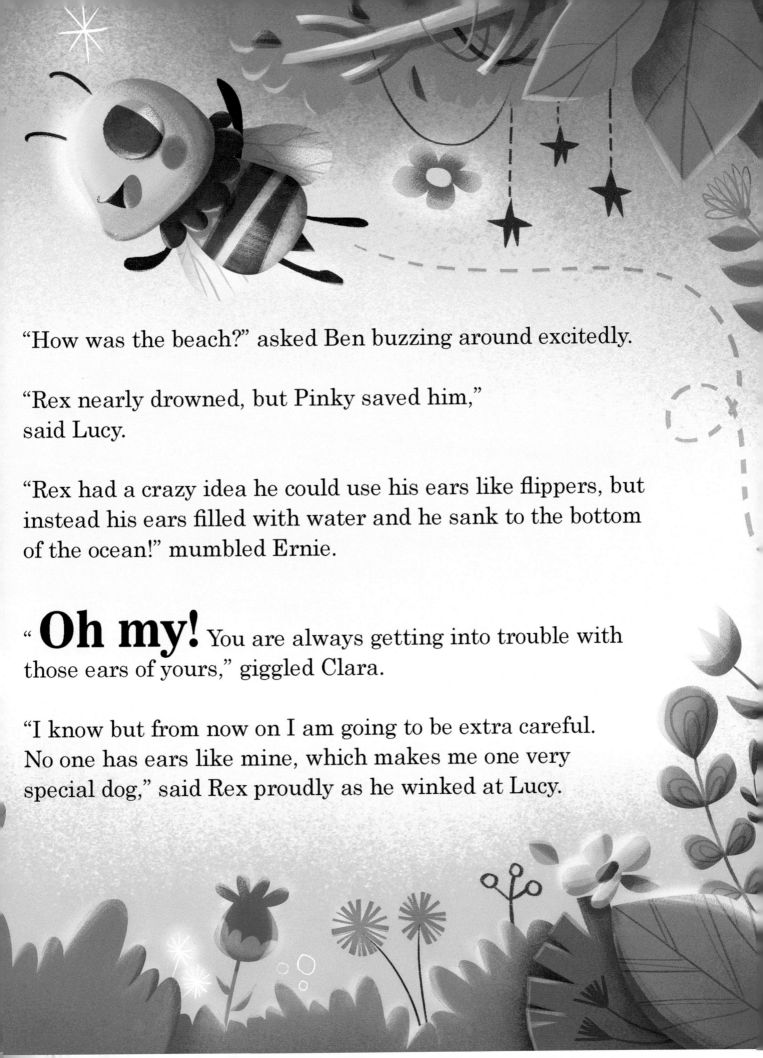

"How was the beach?" asked Ben buzzing around excitedly.

"Rex nearly drowned, but Pinky saved him,"
said Lucy.

"Rex had a crazy idea he could use his ears like flippers, but instead his ears filled with water and he sank to the bottom of the ocean!" mumbled Ernie.

" **Oh my!** You are always getting into trouble with those ears of yours," giggled Clara.

"I know but from now on I am going to be extra careful. No one has ears like mine, which makes me one very special dog," said Rex proudly as he winked at Lucy.

They'd had a wonderful day full of laughter and friendship except for the drama of Rex nearly drowning!

Still nothing in the world was better than when they were all together.

Even though everyone one of them was so different on the outside, they all had one thing in common, being kind and helping their friends.

That's the true meaning of friendship, thought Lucy.

The friends all yawned and rubbed
their eyes at the same time.
It made them giggle — even Ernie.

It was time to go to bed.

They hugged each other tight.

"Good night," said Lucy and Clara.
"Sweet dreams," said Rex.
"Night, night," said Ernie.
"See ya tomorrow dudes," buzzed Ben.

"You are the best friends ever. Good night,"
said Pinky.

Pinky waited until all his friends were asleep.

He tiptoed around the Secret Garden and dug out a wooden box hidden under a rock.

Pinky opened the box and scooped up some magic pinky dust. It shone so brightly and lit up the garden just like a rainbow.

Pinky carefully placed the magic pinky dust in the pockets of his wings.

It was time for Pinky to complete his nightly mission and visit all the children in the world who were tucked up in bed fast asleep.

Pinky took off at the speed of light, high
into the dark starry sky.

"**Wow!** The sky is so beautiful at night.
The stars are so bright and sparkly,"
thought Pinky.

As Pinky flew over all the children's homes he spread
his wings wide and sprinkled his magic pinky dust.

The pinky dust drifted down gently, like snowflakes
travelling along in a cool winters breeze.

The magic pinky dust silently found its way into
each child's room and landed quietly on the floor.

As the sun began to rise Pinky knew his job was done.

All the children were safe, still fast asleep, tucked up in bed surrounded by the magic pinky dust.

The magic pinky dust really was quite special thought Pinky.

Pinky returned home and landed
silently in the Secret Garden.

He tucked in his precious wings, curled into a ball, closed
his eyes and drifted off to sleep taking with him the
secret of his special wings and the magic pinky dust.

But Pinky knew one day he would have to tell all his
friends, the secret of how he got his magic wings and about
the wooden box that held the magic pinky dust.

What would they think of him once
he told them?

Which made Pinky wonder if they too had
their own secret they were hiding?

When you open your eyes in the morning look around and you just might see some of Pinky's magic dust.

Or maybe if you look in the garden, you might find a sprinkling of pinky dust or even the home of Pinky and his friends.

PINKY

Printed in the United States
By Bookmasters